P9-DGB-085

Clifford
The BIG RED DOG

For the real Emily Elizabeth

ISBN 0-590-87957-X

Copyright © 1963, 1985 by Norman Bridwell.
All rights reserved. Published by Scholastic Inc.
CLIFFORD and the CLIFFORD logo are registered trademarks of Scholastic Inc.

12 11 10 9 8 7 6 5 4 3 2 1   6 7 8 9/9 0 1/0

Printed in the U.S.A.   24

Clifford
THE BIG RED DOG

Story and pictures by Norman Bridwell

SCHOLASTIC INC.

New York

I'm Emily Elizabeth,
and I have a dog.

My dog is a big red dog.

Other kids I know have dogs, too.

Some are big dogs.

And some are red dogs.

But I have the biggest, reddest dog on our street.

This is my dog—Clifford.

We have fun together. We play games.

I throw a stick, and he
brings it back to me.

He makes mistakes sometimes.

We play hide-and-seek.

I'm a good hide-and-seek player.

I can find Clifford,

no matter where he hides.

We play camping out,

and I don't need a tent.

He can do tricks, too.

He can sit up and beg.

Oh, I know he's not perfect.

He has *some* bad habits.

He runs after cars.

He catches some of them.

He runs after cats, too.

We don't go to the zoo anymore.

He digs up flowers.

Clifford loves to chew shoes.

It's not easy to keep Clifford.

He eats and drinks a lot.

His house was a problem, too.

But he's a very good watchdog.

The bad boys don't come around anymore.

One day I gave Clifford a bath.

And I combed his hair,
and took him to the dog show.

I'd like to say Clifford won first prize.

But he didn't.

I don't care.

You can keep all your small dogs.

You can keep all your black,

white, brown, and spotted dogs.

I'll keep Clifford . . . . Wouldn't you?